PUFFIN BOOKS

MR BERRY'S ICE-CREAM PARLOUR

Carl is thrilled when Mr Berry comes to stay; Andrew Brimblecombe may have a ten-speed racing bike, but even *he* hasn't got a lodger living in his house. And when Mr Berry announces his plan to open an ice-cream parlour, Carl can hardly believe it. As it turns out, this is just the start of the excitements in store when Mr Berry walks through the door!

Jennifer Zabel is married and lives in Buckinghamshire. She has written several picture books, and *Mr Berry's Ice-Cream Parlour* was her first longer story.

JENNIFER ZABEL

MR BERRY'S ICE-CREAM PARLOUR

ILLUSTRATED BY PATRICIA MacCARTHY

PUFFIN BOOKS

PUFFIN BOOKS

Published by the Penguin Group
27 Wrights Lane, London W8 5TZ, England
Viking Penguin Inc., 40 West 23rd Street, New York, New York 10010, USA
Penguin Books Australia Ltd, Ringwood, Victoria, Australia
Penguin Books Canada Ltd, 2801 John Street, Markham, Ontario, Canada L3R 1B4
Penguin Books (NZ) Ltd, 182–190 Wairau Road, Auckland 10, New Zealand

Penguin Books Ltd, Registered Offices: Harmondsworth, Middlesex, England

First published by Viking Kestrel 1984
Published in Puffin Books 1986
10 9 8 7 6 5 4 3

Made and printed in Great Britain by
Richard Clay Ltd, Bungay, Suffolk
Filmset in Monophoto Palatino

Chapter One

Carl didn't have a father. He lived with his mother in a tall terraced house that looked down over the street at the front, and over lots of other people's backyards and dustbins at the back.

Carl's mother went out to work all day. She worked in the fizzy drinks factory round the corner, as a bottlewasher. She didn't get home until after five o'clock, so Carl had to wear the front-door key on a chain round his neck.

Carl walked home with Andrew Brimblecombe, usually, even if he *was* always showing off about his new ten-speed racing cycle. Andrew was one of those children who are always having new things, or things that are bigger and better than everybody else's. Carl's bicycle was old and rusty, and his mother wouldn't let him ride it any more because she said it was dangerous.

But you can't have everything. Because as soon as they got to Andrew's house after school — it came before Carl's — Andrew would open the front door and Carl would hear Mrs Brimblecombe shriek: 'GET THOSE SHOES OFF BEFORE YOU COME ONE STEP FURTHER!' or: 'WHAT'S THAT ON YOUR TROUSERS?'

So from that point of view, it wasn't so bad not having your mother there when you got home. Sometimes it was awful.

Like the day Carl rushed home with something really, really *exciting* to tell her. It was so exciting he felt sick, and it was all written down on the notes that Mrs Box had handed out at the end of school.

Even though he knew she wasn't there,

Carl raced home as fast as he could, unlocked the door and slammed it behind him. On cold days the house was always warm and welcoming. On hot days, like today, it was cool and quiet.

Carl's plate of biscuits and an apple was on the kitchen table as usual, with a glass of

6 June

Dear Parents,

On 20 August I am planning to take my class on a week's field trip to Sandford, on the South Coast.

We will be staying in a hostel, and the total price will be £25.

Yours sincerely,
P. Box (Mrs)

Please return the slip below

I am willing/unwilling for my child .... to go on the field trip to Sandford, and enclose an initial payment of £5.

Signed ....
(parent/guardian)

orange juice beside it. His mother always put
a large glass bowl over the top of them, to
keep the flies away.

Carl sat down and spread the note out in
front of him, putting his elbows on the table
to study it more closely.

Carl ate his biscuits very slowly, nibbling
them round the edges like a squirrel. He
didn't eat his apple. He put it carefully on top
of the note, like a paperweight.

Then he ran all the way up to his bedroom.
His bed was underneath the window.
Between the tall dark houses he could
just see the rippling green trees of the park,
and the broken-down old hut with its
windows boarded up. In the olden days,
when ladies wore long dresses and carried
parasols, it had been the park tea-room, and a
very smart one, too.

Well, it certainly wasn't smart now. It had
a hole in the roof, for a start.

Carl sat down on the bed, and stared at
the sky. It was deep, and blue, and reminded
him of the sea. Suddenly he couldn't
bear it any longer. He charged downstairs,
grabbed the note, and set off to wait for

his mother outside the fizzy drinks factory.

She was late. She was never late. But today she came hurrying down the steps five minutes after everybody else. She was wearing her brown summer coat over her cotton dress, and her stubby brown umbrella was sticking out of her shopping bag. Carl's mother always took her coat and umbrella to work in the mornings, just in case it was raining when she came out.

'Hello, love!' she exclaimed when she saw Carl standing there. 'I'm sorry I'm late! Did you have a good day at school?'

Carl nodded and suddenly shoved the piece of paper deep into his pocket. It was so important he could hardly bear to show it to her.

Just then an orange-coloured car came out of the factory gates behind them, and Mr Spray, the manager, wound down the window.

'If you change your mind before tomorrow, just give me a buzz, Mrs Anderson!' he called. Mrs Anderson was Carl's mother. 'Hello there, young Carl!'

Then off he zoomed in the opposite direction.

'What did he want, Mum?' asked Carl.

'Oh, nothing important, love,' sighed his mother. 'Mr Spray has an important new client who'll be buying lots of fizzy drinks in future. He's setting up some kind of business and wants to rent a room somewhere near the park.'

'Ooh!' gasped Carl. 'Did Mr Spray ask if he could rent a room in *our* house?'

'Well yes, he did,' said Carl's mother. 'He knows I could do with a bit of extra money. The trouble is, your home's not your own when you've got a lodger. You're always having to say good morning and good evening when you pass on the stairs. So I said no.'

'Oh,' said Carl, disappointed. Then, 'Mum, I've brought a note home from school. Do you want to read it? I think it's about a kind of holiday, or something.'

Carl's mother rumpled his hair and read the note.

'Oh, Carl! It's a lot of money, love. I don't know whether I can afford it this year!'

Carl felt his heart fall straight into his shoes. He'd never thought about the money. Silly him, why hadn't he thought about the *money*?

They walked on in silence. Carl squeezed his mother's hand and studied the cracks in the pavement. He spotted a five pence piece which he picked up and pretended to polish. He hoped he wasn't going to cry. Not out in the street, that would be really stupid. And his mother would feel awful.

Then, at the corner where the telephone box was, his mother suddenly stopped. She ~~~d around in her purse and frowned.

'Carl,' she said. 'Can I have that five pence piece you've just found?'

Carl nodded miserably.

'Cheer up, love!' she said briskly. 'I'm going to phone Mr Spray and tell him I've changed my mind. He'll be home by now.'

Carl stared at her.

'You mean, we're going to have a lodger?'

'Yes, if we think he's nice enough. And *you*, young fellow my lad, are going on that field trip with the school this summer!'

Carl was so happy and excited he nearly burst. Instead, he and his mother squeezed into the telephone box to phone Mr Spray . . .

' . . . Oh! Oh my goodness me! Well, we'd better be off then. Goodbye, Mr Spray, see you in the morning,' said Carl's mother in a terrible hurry.

'What's the matter?' asked Carl anxiously.

'Mr Berry is coming round at seven o'clock this evening! I'll have to spring-clean the kitchen!'

Off she hurried down the street. She was so flustered she even put her umbrella up! Carl thought he'd never stop laughing.

He jogged along beside her, his eyes sparkling.

'Mum!' he said. 'Isn't it funny how that five pence piece happened to be lying there, just when we needed it? That was really lucky!'

Chapter Two

On the way home they bought fish and chips
for tea, to save time. Afterwards Carl's
mother wished she hadn't, in case the lodger
didn't like the smell of fish and chips.

Then Carl swept the kitchen floor while
his mother scrubbed the kitchen sink.

'Where will he sleep, anyway?' asked Carl.

'In the spare room, next to you,' replied
his mother, wiping a blob of foam off her
nose. 'We'll have to take all the junk down
into the cellar.'

'Now?' asked Carl, hopefully.

'No, not now,' replied his mother, looking
at the clock and taking her apron off. 'Mr
Berry will be here soon. I'll just go and tidy

myself up a bit. You go and plump the cushions up in the sitting room.'

Carl plumped the cushions up in the sitting room. Then he picked one up again and rolled around on the rug, hugging it.

'Andrew Brimblecombe hasn't got a lodger!' he thought gleefully. 'Even if he *does* have a ten-speed racing cycle!'

Carl's mother came down again, looking very nice in her best pink summer dress. She was even wearing little white earrings.

'Carl, you're covered in bits off the rug!' she cried. 'Go and change your jumper!'

But it was too late for Carl to change his jumper. Someone was knocking on the door. His mother quickly patted her hair tidy and walked down the hall to open the front door.

Carl dawdled behind picking bits of rug off his jumper.

'Good evening, Mrs Anderson,' said a deep, friendly voice.

Carl peeped up through his lashes and saw

Mr Berry. He had a round, cheerful face with
lots of curly ginger hair that looked as frothy
as the bubbles on top of a milkshake.

'Your hair's as frothy as a milkshake!' said
Carl before he could stop himself.

'Oh!' gasped his mother, horrified.

Mr Berry examined himself closely in the hall mirror. 'You're quite right, it is!' he declared.

Carl's mother just went on looking horrified.

'Don't worry!' laughed Mr Berry. 'In my line of business it doesn't matter if you go around looking like a milkshake!'

'Why?' asked Carl.

'Now stop pestering Mr Berry!' scolded his mother, getting all flustered again.

Mr Berry winked. 'I'll tell you later!' he whispered to Carl, following Mrs Anderson into the kitchen.

'We had a spring-clean in here for you!' Carl announced.

'Carl!' cried his mother, her face turning as pink as her best summer dress.

Carl's mother showed Mr Berry all over the house, ending up with the spare room.

'Why, this is splendid!' declared Mr Berry. 'When can I move in?'

Carl looked anxiously at his mother. You never knew with mothers. *He* thought that Mr Berry was great. *She* might think he was the worst person in the world.

'Tomorrow, if you like!' she said.

'Splendid!' said Mr Berry, rolling up his shirt sleeves.

And for the next half-hour everybody staggered up and down to the cellar with boxes of books, old lampshades, Carl's old baby toys and the holiday suitcases.

When they'd finished Carl's mother made some tea and carried it into the sitting room on a tray.

There was a plate of ginger biscuits, too. That reminded Carl about Mr Berry's curly ginger hair. It must have reminded Mr Berry as well, because he said: 'Ah yes. My hair. Well, it's quite all right for me to have milkshake hair, Carl, because I'm going to open an ice-cream parlour soon. I'll be selling ice-creams, fizzy drinks — and milkshakes, too!'

AN ICE-CREAM PARLOUR!

Carl could hardly believe his ears. How absolutely, fantastically *marvellous*!

'Can I help you, sometimes?' he asked, in a very small voice.

'Certainly!' cried Mr Berry. 'The more the

merrier! In fact, I shall be needing quite a lot of help *before* I open the ice-cream parlour, too!'

'Why?' asked Carl, doing a big bounce on the armchair.

'Well,' began Mr Berry slowly, taking a ginger biscuit. 'You know that broken-down old hut in the park? The one with the windows boarded up and the hole in the roof? *That* is going to be my ice-cream parlour!'

The next day Mr Berry moved in. He was taking suitcases and boxes out of a little red car when Carl rushed home from school.

Carl looked at all Mr Berry's possessions on the pavement. He was amazed they could all have come out of that one small car.

'Is that your car?' he asked.

'It most certainly is!' declared Mr Berry. 'We'll ride round and make a start on my future premises in a minute, if you like.'

Round they went to the park, with mops

and brushes sticking out of the window of the little red car. They passed Andrew Brimblecombe on the way, showing off on his new ten-speed racer.

'That's Andrew Brimblecombe,' Carl told Mr Berry. 'That's his new bike.'

'I see,' said Mr Berry.

'I'll take the boards off the windows first,' said Mr Berry when they arrived at the old hut. But before that he took the padlock off the door so that Carl could go inside.

It was dark and dusty in there, with just one patch of light that came from the hole in the roof. Carl's nose began to tickle. But outside Mr Berry had got to work with his pliers. One by one, the boards came off the windows and sunshine flooded into the hut. Carl looked round and saw a dusty counter, cupboards with their doors hanging off, a stack of dingy tables and chairs and a few tattered parasols standing in a corner.

'What a mess!' exclaimed Mr Berry,

appearing in the doorway. 'Never mind, the sooner we get started, the sooner we can get to the interesting bit.'

'What's the interesting bit?' asked Carl, who secretly thought it was all interesting.

'Painting everything in ice-cream colours!' said Mr Berry.

'I'll get started on the tables and chairs, then!' said Carl quickly.

He filled the bucket at the sink and poured in lots of soap powder. Then he carried the tables and chairs outside, one by one, and gave each one a really good scrub.

Carl looked up and saw Mr Berry perched on the roof, mending the hole.

'Can I come up?' he asked eagerly.

'Certainly not!' exclaimed Mr Berry. 'I've been on rooftops before, my lad, and you haven't! Besides, you're doing a grand job on those tables and chairs!'

They were late home for tea. Mr Berry felt very bad about it because it was his first day. But Carl's mother just looked at their grubby faces and smiled.

'I hope you like sausages and treacle pudding, Mr Berry,' she said.

'That's my favourite meal, Mrs Anderson!'

exclaimed Mr Berry. 'How did you guess?' And off he went to wash his hands, shaking his head in amazement.

'Is it really his favourite meal, or is he just saying that?' asked Carl.

'I don't know, love,' said Mrs Anderson happily. 'But I don't think it really matters, does it?'

Chapter Three

It took Carl and Mr Berry a whole week to clean and repair the hut.

They'd work until a quarter to five, then pick Carl's mother up from work. One day she asked Mr Berry to drive them straight back to the park instead of home for tea. Then she sat down on the grass, opened her shopping bag — and took out a lovely picnic. She'd been out shopping in her lunch hour.

Afterwards Mr Berry went to sleep with a big red and white handkerchief over his face.

Mrs Anderson tiptoed into the hut and took a tape measure out of her pocket to measure the windows.

'I'm going to make some curtains as a

surprise for Mr Berry,' she whispered. 'What colour do you think I should get?'

'Oh, ice-cream colour, I should think,' said Carl airily.

The day after the picnic Mr Berry took Carl to buy all the ice-cream-coloured paint.

They decided on eight cans of strawberry pink paint, six cans of minty green paint, four cans of milk chocolate paint, two cans of cream paint and one can of white paint. They also bought a supply of paint brushes, all different sizes, with gleaming black bristles.

Then they set to work. Mr Berry said they wouldn't bother with a plan. Then the whole thing would look natural. Carl started off with a can of milk chocolate paint, and when he got tired of that, he opened a can of strawberry pink paint instead.

When it was all done, Carl and Mr Berry stepped back to admire their handiwork.

'Excellent!' declared Mr Berry. 'A most pleasing neapolitan effect, don't you think?'

Carl nodded happily. He'd never seen anything so lovely in his life.

'Tomorrow we'll paint the tables and chairs,' continued Mr Berry on the way home. Then he gave a deep sigh. 'After that we'll have to go and choose some curtain

material. I hate choosing curtain material!'

Carl bit his lip and looked away.

That evening, when Mr Berry was busy
reading his newspaper in the sitting room,
Carl's mother took him upstairs to see the
curtain material. There was heaps and heaps

of it, because she'd bought enough to make new covers for the parasols, too. It was a bright yellow colour, with tiny strawberries all over it.

Carl thought it was just right.

On Saturday morning, a van delivered all the equipment for the ice-cream parlour.

There were two enormous fridges and lots of steel bowls and jugs, clear and shiny as mirrors. There were piles of pretty glass dishes with edges like petals. They came separated from one another by pieces of soft, crumpled tissue paper so that they wouldn't break on the way. There were sets of tall glasses for milkshakes and ice-cream sundaes, and boxes of spoons with long handles for reaching to the bottom of the tall glasses.

As it was a Saturday, Carl's mother was there to help stack everything away.

Afterwards she handed Mr Berry a big package with all the crisp new curtains and frilly parasol covers in it. Mr Berry was

delighted, and gave her a big kiss.

'That settles it!' he announced. 'I shall open my ice-cream parlour next Saturday!'

Carl felt sick with excitement. He told everyone in his class, including Mrs Box, to come and try one of Mr Berry's ice-creams on opening day.

'Pooh!' went Andrew Brimblecombe. 'I bet they're *awful*. Especially if he's never made any before!'

'He has, so there, lots of times!' cried Carl. 'And even if he hasn't, they'll taste nice. Mr Berry never makes a mess of *anything*!'

But secretly Carl thought it wouldn't do any harm to keep his fingers crossed on opening day. Just in case.

As it happened, Mr Berry's ice-creams were not *awful*. In fact, not only were they not *awful*, they were the most delicious, creamy, melt-on-your-tongue yummy ice-creams that *anyone*, even *Andrew Brimblecombe*, had ever tasted!

'You can uncross your fingers now, Carl!' grinned Mr Berry, scooping up different-coloured balls of ice-cream as fast as he could go.

Carl blushed with embarrassment, and wondered how Mr Berry had known.

Outside, Carl's mother was flitting about between the parasols taking orders. She was wearing a little apron that she'd made out of a left-over piece of material.

Andrew Brimblecombe was sitting at one table with his parents and little brother William.

'What delicious coconut ice-cream!' cooed Mrs Brimblecombe. '*Very* unusual! *William!* You've got a big blob of butterscotch ice-cream on the seat of your dungarees!'

Andrew looked sideways at Carl, and they grinned at each other.

Mrs Box was there, too, with her husband. It was always interesting to see who your teacher was married to. Mr Box was probably very nice, thought Carl, because as soon as Mrs Box had finished her first ice-cream sundae, he bought her another one.

Mr Berry was so busy that he put Carl in charge of the cornets. He stood at his own window with his own scoop to dig balls of ice-cream out with, and a squeezy bottle of chocolate sauce so that you could have a dollop of chocolate on top of your cornet.

When they got home that evening, they

were all tired out. Carl's mother made beans on toast for tea, and Mr Berry did the washing up.

Before Carl went to sleep that night, he sat looking out of the window with his quilt around him. Between the tall dark houses he could see the green of the park, and the bright little blob that was Mr Berry's ice-cream parlour. Then he lay down, so that he could only see the sky.

The clouds looked just like twirly-whirly ice-cream cornets.

Chapter Four

When the summer holidays came Carl spent every day at the ice-cream parlour with Mr Berry.

They weren't always as busy as they had been on that first Saturday, especially on weekdays. Sometimes they had time to sit and have a game of chess or Scrabble at one of the little tables. Mr Berry had a very nice chess set that he would bring over to the ice-cream parlour with him. The pieces were made of marble, one set as white as moonlight and the other as black as the blackest midnight.

'These chess pieces sort of *sing*,' announced Carl one day. He would have felt

silly saying that to some people, but not to
Mr Berry.

'What do you mean?' asked Mr Berry,
putting his head on one side.

'I don't mean they actually *sing*,' said Carl.
'It's just that they're so nice that when I look
at them and touch them – it's as if I can hear
somebody singing in a very high voice.'

'I know exactly what you mean,' nodded Mr Berry. 'I sometimes hear that singing voice when I'm walking through very tall trees and the sun is shining through them.'

'Er, checkmate, Mr Berry,' said Carl.

'Oh dear, so it is,' sighed Mr Berry, looking at his watch. 'Come on then, Carl! Closing time! And you'd better be home in good time to help your mother with the packing!'

'What packing?' frowned Carl.

'You're setting off on your school trip tomorrow. Had you forgotten?'

Carl had forgotten. The awful thing was that he wasn't sure if he wanted to go on it now. To start with he'd never been away from home before, and he had a funny feeling that Mr Berry and the ice-cream parlour might have vanished by the time he got back.

He sat on his bed swinging his legs and watching his mother pack his things. When she'd finished she slipped a big bar of chocolate in as a surprise for when he got there. Carl pretended not to notice.

The next morning they all drove round to the school and Carl's mother and Mr Berry stayed to wave goodbye to the bus. Carl watched his suitcase being strapped to the roof-rack with everybody else's. He'd *have* to go now.

His mother gave him a big kiss. 'In you get, love, or you won't get a seat by the window!'

'Are you sure you can manage the ice-cream parlour without me?' he asked Mr Berry gruffly.

'Well, I'll tell you one thing,' declared Mr Berry, putting his finger on the end of Carl's nose. 'It'll still be there when you get back! And we'll still be here, too, standing right here on this very spot!'

Carl had a marvellous week at the seaside. They went out on lobster boats, studied rock

pools, got up very early one morning to visit
the fish market, and spent a whole afternoon
at a ruined cliff-top castle. They drew two
pictures of it in their sketch pads, one of it in
ruins as it was now, and one of how they
imagined it might have been in olden times.

In the evenings they had hot chocolate or orange juice and biscuits for supper, then settled down to read, or write their postcards.

'Dear Mummy and Mr Berry,' began Carl. 'We are having a smashing time. The food is great. Tonight we had sausages, chips and baked beans for dinner, with apple pie and custard. It was great, except for the custard which had lumps in it. Andrew Brimblecombe likes lumps so he had mine. We went to the fish market. It was very interesting and smelly. Love Carl x x x'

It seemed strange, writing 'Mrs C. Anderson and Mr Berry' on the address side. He could hardly fit it on. He wondered what Mr Berry's first name was. 'C' stood for Caroline.

When he did get home, Mr Berry and his mother were waiting for the bus, exactly where they said they would be.

'Have you been standing there all week?'

asked Carl in delight, jumping off the bus and hugging them.

'Not *all* week!' joked Mr Berry. 'We did pop off for *one* afternoon. To get married.'

Carl opened his eyes and his mouth as wide as they would go.

Then, 'YIPPEE!' he went.

After that, things changed quite a lot. Carl's mother stopped working at the fizzy drinks factory, for one thing, because she wanted to help in the ice-cream parlour.

Mr Spray, the manager, was very sad to see her go, and said jokingly that it was all his fault for introducing her to Mr Berry in the first place. Everybody in the factory clubbed together and bought them a cuckoo clock as a wedding present.

The second thing was that Mr Berry had moved out of the spare room and was now sleeping with Carl's mother in her big double bed with the billowing eiderdown.

'Thank goodness I'll have someone to help

keep this big bed warm in winter!' she
laughed.

It was only just autumn, but people were
already beginning to think about winter.
When Carl went back to school after the
holidays, he went in his winter uniform.

The first leaves fell from the trees in the

park and drifted over the tables of the
ice-cream parlour. The fringes of the parasols
shivered.

Then one breakfast time, Mr Berry folded
his newspaper and sighed.

'Well, Carl!' he said. 'Today's the day!'

'What for?' asked Carl.

'Packing up the ice-cream parlour for the
winter,' replied his new father. 'An ice-cream
is the *last* thing anybody wants in the
winter!'

'Can't we sell hot dogs and tea, instead?'
cried Carl in desperation. He couldn't
imagine what life would be like without the
ice-cream parlour.

'I'm afraid not, Carl,' said Mr Berry,
shaking his head regretfully. 'You see, I've
got a different job for the winter. A post
office job. All that extra Christmas post, you
know.'

Carl bit his lip, and smashed his boiled egg
on the top, very hard.

'Carl!' said his mother. 'What on earth is the matter with you?'

Well, Carl knew there was no point trying to explain that Andrew Brimblecombe had his ten-speed racer and he, Carl, had the ice-cream parlour, except that now Andrew Brimblecombe still had his racer but he, Carl, didn't have anything, or *felt* that he didn't have anything ... well, there was no point in trying to explain all that. Especially when Carl felt a bit ashamed of feeling like that.

'Nothing!' he muttered, trailing upstairs to clean his teeth.

'Carl, I'm setting off for the ice-cream parlour in ten minutes,' said Mr Berry, popping his head round the bathroom door. 'I'll need your help to carry all the tables and chairs inside.'

'All right,' mumbled Carl through a mouthful of toothpaste. But he didn't look at Mr Berry. He just went on cleaning his teeth

and looking at his funny, sad face in the cold water tap.

It was a dismal job, packing up the ice-cream parlour. The worst thing of all was boarding up the windows and putting the padlock on the door.

They walked slowly back to the car, Carl scuffling up the leaves with his new winter shoes.

'I like winter,' said Mr Berry, presently. 'It sparkles.'

Carl was silent for a while. 'Are you any good at sledging, Mr Berry?'

'Who, *me*?' exclaimed Mr Berry, nudging Carl on the shoulder in a teasing kind of way. 'Faster than the speed of light on a sledge, I am!'

Carl imagined himself and Mr Berry beating Andrew Brimblecombe and his father in a sledge race.

'Good!' he said.

Chapter Five

For a long time Mr Berry wasn't very busy with the post. He spent a lot of his time digging the back garden for spring vegetables. He also planted hundreds of bulbs and a little pear tree that was nothing but twigs.

For the front of the house, where there wasn't a garden at all, really, just a few flagstones, he bought a big earthenware pot and filled that with bulbs too. But in the middle he planted a little evergreen tree, so that there would be something green in the pot all the year round. It was a little fir tree, the shape of a candle flame.

At the weekends the whole family went

on long walks in the countryside. Carl
and Mr Berry took turns at carrying the
haversack with the picnic in it.

'Now it's no good going for all these hikes
unless we're properly kitted out!' declared
Mr Berry. 'We'll all end up with wet feet and
blisters!' And so saying, he marched them all
down to the nearest outdoor shop to buy
sturdy hiking boots.

'Oh dear! I don't look very elegant in these, do I?' said Carl's mother, doubtfully.

'Nonsense!' declared Mr Berry.

He wasn't going to let them be put off by the weather, either. They all had to buy plastic macs to take with them. He absolutely *refused* to let Carl's mother take her umbrella with her.

Once, not very far from the town, they began to follow a little woodland path that seemed somehow still and special. Carl stopped chattering, and walked quietly along through the lacy arches of trees. He found himself peering hard down the long avenues of tree trunks, almost as if he expected to see someone approaching.

Suddenly he noticed a thick tangle of blackberry bushes, and left the pathway to see if he could find any blackberries. There were lots of them, all very big, purple and juicy.

He was just about to call to the others

when something made him stop. It wasn't a
sound exactly, it was more like the opposite
of a sound. A sudden, magical silence. And
then he saw it.

A deer. Standing beyond the blackberry
thicket in a pale golden shaft of sunlight.

'Oh, you lovely thing!' whispered Carl. All the magic of the woodland seemed to come from that beautiful wild creature as it gazed, just like a god of the forest, right into Carl's eyes.

Then it was gone. Though which way it had bounded Carl had no idea.

'I saw a deer!' he cried, rushing back through the crackly carpet of leaves. 'The most beautiful deer in the world, with antlers!'

'Oh, Carl!' laughed his mother. 'There are no deer in this wood, love, I'm sure!'

'Well, I wouldn't know about that!' protested Mr Berry, holding his chin in his hand and nodding his head thoughtfully. 'After all, how well do you know this wood, my dear?'

And Carl's mother had to admit that she'd never been there before, so who was she to say?

'What's the name of the wood, I wonder?'

mused Mr Berry. 'Have a quick look at the map, Carl.'

Eagerly Carl spread the map out on the dry forest floor. 'Gat's Wood, it's called,' he said, feeling disappointed. He'd hoped it might have been something like Deer Forest.

'I suppose Gat was a farmer who owned the wood once upon a time,' suggested Carl's mother.

'Could be, could be!' said Mr Berry. 'But then again, if you read "Gat's " the other way round ...'

And with that, off he strode along the woodland path, humming cheerfully and staring up into the branches as if he were looking for squirrels.

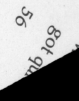

Chapter Six

Mr Berry began his winter postman's job at
the beginning of November. Off he would
go with his packed lunch, his hiking boots, a
black raincoat and a peaked cap. He even
took the map with him, Carl noticed.

'Some of these postboxes are in the
middle of nowhere!' he told Carl, as he set off
at six o'clock one morning. Carl was sitting
on the bottom step in his dressing-gown.
'Sometimes I trudge for miles up a dirt track,
and there's only one letter waiting for me at
the end of it!'

But he didn't seem to mind. He liked
working out of doors, he said, and his face
~~was~~ quite weatherbeaten.

The good thing about being a postman, of course, is that although you have to start work early in the mornings, you usually come home early in the afternoons.

Mr Berry did. When Carl got home from school, he was usually making toast at the fireside, and everywhere smelt of toast and jam.

They would sit by the fire and eat it, and then have a game of chess or Scrabble, just like they used to at the ice-cream parlour.

Carl's mother would usually come in and have some toast and jam with them, but after that she was usually busy making the dinner.

It was late one November afternoon, when Mrs Box was giving them a history lesson and the classroom was hot and smelled of chalk dust and school dinner, that the first snow fell. Soft and powerful, down it fell. The children cheered, then gazed, entranced.

It seemed ages till half past three.

'Very well, off you go!' sighed Mrs Box at two minutes to half past. Kind Mrs Box. Carl and Andrew had a snowball fight on the way home. Carl aimed a beauty at Andrew just as he was about to open his

front door. But unfortunately Mrs Brimblecombe opened the door first.

'TAKE THOSE SHOES OFF IMMED –' she began.

Then Carl's snowball hit her smack in the face.

Carl shot round the corner and up his own front steps. Mr Berry was nowhere to be seen. His mother was in the kitchen, peeling potatoes.

'Hi, Mum, where's Mr Berry?' demanded Carl.

'Hello, love. Your father's down in the cellar, doing something to your sledge.'

'What's he doing to it? I'm going to ask him if he'll come out sledging with me today!'

Down into the cellar he raced, leaving his mother still peeling potatoes. Mr Berry was polishing the runners of the sledge, to get the rust off.

'Come out sledging with me now, before dinner!' cried Carl, excitedly.

'Why not?' smiled Mr Berry.

There was one particular slope in the park that was the world's best place for sledging. Carl and Mr Berry trudged along through the snow, pulling the sledge behind them. When they got as far as the ice-cream parlour, Carl drew a round smiling face in the snow that was clinging to the door.

Andrew Brimblecombe was already there, showing off with a brand-new bright yellow sledge that didn't have any runners.

'No *runners!*' sniffed Mr Berry under his breath. 'A sledge isn't a sledge without *runners!* Come on Carl, you get on and I'll sit behind.'

Perhaps it was because Mr Berry was heavier, or perhaps it was because he'd polished the runners, but the sledge shot down the slope like a dream. It flew like a bird, faster than it had ever done before.

Andrew stared down at them from the top of the slope.

'I'll bring *my* dad tomorrow, and we'll race
you!' he yelled, as Carl and Mr Berry started
up the slope again. When they were halfway
up he whizzed past them, a streak of yellow
that shrieked like a banshee.

'You will come, won't you?' asked Carl, eagerly.

'I'll try to, Carl, but I can't promise,' said Mr Berry. 'I've had to bring a great pile of Christmas post home to sort out tonight. And tomorrow it will be even worse. It's the snow, you see, it makes everyone feel Christmassy!'

When they got home, Carl's mother was just about to take the dinner out of the oven. She looked hot and tired.

'We had a super-duper time, didn't we, Mr Berry?' said Carl, plonking himself down at the table.

After dinner Mr Berry shut himself up in the dining room with his work.

'Will you have a game of Scrabble with me tonight, Mr Berry?' Carl asked from the doorway. The table was snowed under with letters and cards.

'No time tonight, son!' said Mr Berry, turning round to look at him in the lamplight. He had his spectacles on. 'Why don't you ask your mother?'

'Oh, she can't play Scrabble half as well as you can!' shrugged Carl.

'Is that so?' said Mr Berry, thoughtfully. 'Well then, Carl, you'll just have to do without a game tonight, won't you?'

'S'pose so!' sighed Carl, trailing up to bed.

The whole of the next day he was very excited, thinking about the sledge race. He raced home from school as fast as he could, to get ready for it.

Mr Berry was lying on the bed. Fast asleep.

'He's so tired he fell asleep the minute he came home,' whispered Carl's mother. 'But I'm sure he wouldn't mind if you woke him up for the sledge race!'

Carl looked at Mr Berry. He had a blue patchwork blanket over his legs, and his feet were sticking out in their woolly postman's socks.

'It doesn't matter,' he muttered
mournfully. 'If I was so tired that I fell asleep
in the middle of the afternoon, I think I'd feel
awful if somebody woke me up.'

His mother put her hand on his drooping
shoulder.

'I know it's not the same,' she began, 'but I
could come.'

Carl looked at her, astonished.

'Oh, great, Mum!' he cried. 'But you'll have
to put your trousers on. It's a pretty cold
business, sledging!'

By the time she'd finished muffling herself
up, Carl's mother had disappeared
completely. She could even have been the
Abominable Snowman.

'How do you do, Mr Berry?' said Andrew
Brimblecombe's father, stamping around in
the snow to keep his feet warm.

Carl and Andrew decided to go for the
best of three. To Carl's delight he and his
mother won the first race easily. But the

second time they both tumbled off into the
snow, and the sledge went careering off
without them.

'Tough luck!' grinned Andrew, struggling
back up the slope with both sledges in tow
and his face as red as a beetroot.

'Just keep your head down and hang on!'
whispered Carl's mother, as they lined up for
the last race of all. And this time they went
like the wind, and it was Andrew and his
father who ended up in a flurry of snow.

'Oh Carl, that was wonderful!' laughed
Carl's mother breathlessly. 'I haven't had so
much fun for a long time!'

Carl was very quiet.

When they got home, the tea was made.
There was a plate of home-made scones, just
out of the oven, some strawberry jam in a
little glass dish, and three boiled eggs under
little egg cosies.

'Oh, what a lovely surprise!' cried Carl's
mother in delight.

Mr Berry was nowhere to be seen. Carl
suspected he'd hopped straight back to
bed when he heard them coming. He went
upstairs and opened the bedroom door
just wide enough to see through. Mr Berry
was lying on the bed with his eyes shut.

He opened one, and looked at Carl with it.

'Who won?' he asked.

'We did,' said Carl, with his mouth against the crack. Then he grinned, and Mr Berry grinned, too. 'Are you coming down for tea now?'

'You bet!' cried Mr Berry, leaping off the bed. 'Let's see if I can make scones as well as your mother can sledge, shall we?'

He couldn't.

Chapter Seven

'What shall I do, Mum?' asked Carl, a couple of weeks before Christmas. He didn't see much of Mr Berry these days. Every evening he came home from work and just disappeared into the dining room, which he'd taken over as his office. He only came out for meals, and to go to bed.

'Why don't you make some Christmas cards?' replied his mother. She was very good at coming up with just the right idea, was Carl's mother.

She stood on a chair and took a big, flat chocolate box out of a top cupboard.

'Here you are!' she said. 'All last year's

birthday cards and Christmas cards for you to cut up.'

Carl ran up to his bedroom and took out some sheets of coloured paper, a pair of scissors and the glue. Then he settled down at his little table and set to work.

Soon he had six Christmas cards standing

on the window sill. Next came the hard bit. Making the envelopes. He'd just started to write the names on them, when his mother came in with a glass of orange juice and a chocolate biscuit.

'Mum, what's Mr Berry's first name?' he asked. His mother always called him 'dear', or 'darling'.

'Nicholas,' replied his mother. 'But you can call him Daddy, or Dad, if you like.'

'I know I can,' said Carl, writing 'Mr N. Berry' very carefully on the envelope.

When he'd finished Carl came downstairs and put the two cards, his mother's and Mr Berry's, on the doormat. Suddenly he heard someone coming up the cellar steps, and out came an old brown suitcase followed by Mr Berry.

'Oh,' said Mr Berry. 'Hello, Carl. Guess what. I've got to go away for a week or so. Up to postal headquarters. They're very busy up there this year, can't cope.'

'But you'll be back for Christmas, won't you?' asked Carl, anxiously.

'That I *can* promise!' declared Mr Berry. 'Now then, where can I find a duster to dust off this old suitcase?'

'In the duster bag in the broom cupboard,' said Carl. Mr Berry knew exactly where the dusters were kept. 'When are you going?'

'Tomorrow morning!' called Mr Berry from the broom cupboard. 'And by the way, you haven't told me what you want for Christmas, yet!'

'You haven't told me what *you'd* like, either!' replied Carl, leaning against the wall with his hands in his pockets. 'Anyway, there's something lying on the mat.'

That night, Carl's mother roasted chestnuts in the hearth. On the mantelpiece were lots of Christmas cards, including one from Andrew Brimblecombe.

'I think I'll go and do some Christmas shopping tomorrow, Mum,' said Carl,

suddenly. 'I'll see if Andrew wants to come with me.'

'Good idea!' His mother was pleased. She was kneeling on the rug, getting the chestnuts out with the poker. 'I'll treat you both to a milkshake and a sticky bun, if you like!'

'And I could give you a lift into town on my way!' added Mr Berry, who was having a night off from work because he was going away the next day.

'Thanks, Dad!' said Carl.

At nine o'clock the next morning Mr Berry threw his old brown suitcase into the car, kissed Carl's mother on the cheek, and got into the driver's seat. Then he parped on the horn for Carl, who was counting his money on the hall table.

'Here's two pounds for your milkshakes, or whatever,' sniffed his mother, wiping her eyes on her apron. Carl gave her a quick hug, raced down the steps, and hopped in beside Mr Berry.

First they zipped round to Andrew Brimblecombe's house. Mrs Brimblecombe was just bringing the milk in from the front step. She was wearing a bright purple dressing-gown, and her head was covered with jumbo-sized hair curlers, with spikes sticking out of them.

'Yoo hoo, Mr Berry!' called Mrs Brimblecombe, waving cheerily.

'Go and fetch your friend, fast!' hissed Mr Berry under his breath. 'Morning, Mrs Brimblecombe! Nearly Christmas!'

Carl and Andrew were back in a trice. Carl

sat in the front, beside his father. Andrew sat in the back.

Andrew's father had a car, too. It was much bigger than Mr Berry's, and Andrew's father spent most Sunday afternoons lying underneath it. Carl wondered if he really was mending it, or just hiding from Mrs Brimblecombe.

'This car goes very fast, for a little car!' said Andrew admiringly, as they zoomed into town.

Mr Berry dropped the boys off outside Muff's, the big department store. Its windows were hung with golden tinsel and huge velvet balls on red ribbons.

'Bye, Dad!' said Carl, with a lump in his throat. 'By the way, I've decided what I want for Christmas!'

'DON'T TELL ME! Let's see if I can guess!' laughed Carl's father, leaning over and smiling up at him. 'Goodbye, son, see you at Christmas!' Then he wound up the window, gave a cheery wave of his hand, and sped away into the traffic.

'What are you going to get for your mum?' asked Andrew, as they stepped on to the soft blue carpets of the department store. They were in the bit that sells lipsticks and things, and there was a warm, heavy smell of perfumes and powders.

'I don't know yet,' said Carl. 'How much is perfume?'

They looked at the prices and their eyes nearly popped out of their heads.

'I haven't got that much money to spend on everybody put together!' said Andrew.

'Neither have I,' said Carl.

A big sign above a flight of steps read: TO BARGAIN BASEMENT. So down they went. There were all sorts of things for sale down in the Bargain Basement. After a long think Carl decided to buy his mother a china thimble. It was very pretty, with a tiny pink rose painted on the top.

'I know she'll like it,' he said, as the smiling lady assistant looked around for a tiny box to put it in. 'I've never *ever* bought her a present that wasn't *exactly* what she's always wanted.'

'Hey, that's funny!' exclaimed Andrew. 'Neither have I! I'm going to buy her a pincushion this year.'

The pincushion he chose was in the shape of a hedgehog, and the pins were supposed to be the spikes. Carl said he thought it was the perfect present for Mrs Brimblecombe.

'I'm getting my dad a torch!' continued Andrew. 'Because I'm always borrowing his and losing it.'

It took Carl ages to decide what to buy for Mr Berry. In the end he bought him a pair of big red woolly mittens, to keep his hands warm when he was out doing the post.

Then, as it was nearly ten o'clock, they decided to go and have their elevenses in the

snack bar. Carl had a raspberry milkshake and
a jam doughnut. Andrew had a banana
milkshake and a vanilla slice. He said the
milkshake wasn't half as nice as Mr Berry's.

'What shall we do now?' Carl said
afterwards.

'Go and get my little brother a present,'
replied Andrew, slurping up the rest of his
milkshake through his straw.

Carl didn't have a little brother to buy a present for, but he helped choose a nice furry rabbit for Andrew's brother William. It would be just small enough to fit inside the pocket of his dungarees.

Chapter Eight

It was the day before Christmas and Carl was helping his mother do the Christmas baking. Afterwards, in the late afternoon, they would trim the tree and put up the paperchains in the sitting room.

'I expect Dad will be home today!' said Carl cheerfully. He was scraping the bowl with his finger for all the left-over chocolate from the chocolate buns.

'I'm afraid he won't be back until early on Christmas morning, love!' said his mother.

'Bother!' said Carl. 'He won't be able to help trim the tree. And what about the Christmas cake?'

Carl and his mother always cut the first

slice of Christmas cake on Christmas Eve. It was their special Christmas tradition.

'I suppose we could wait until Christmas Day!' said Carl, doubtfully.

'Nonsense!' said his mother. 'We'll cut the cake tonight, just as we've always done. But I tell you what we *could* do. We could save the first slice for your father, and leave it with a glass of ginger wine for when he comes in tonight. We'll both be fast asleep by then, I expect!'

'Great idea, Mum!' Carl cheered up. 'Shall we do the mince pies now?'

After lunch they treated themselves to a mince pie each, still warm from the oven. They tasted delicious.

'Why don't we go and pick some holly this afternoon?' suggested Carl's mother suddenly, when they'd finished washing up.

'Ooh, yes!' cried Carl. 'Let's go on the bus to Gat's Wood! I bet there'll be lots of holly there!'

They travelled upstairs on the bus, and it wasn't long before they could see the misty grey outline of Gat's Wood in the distance.

There *was* lots of holly there, with bright red berries and dark, glossy leaves sparkling with frost. But there was no deer. Carl looked and looked, but he knew that he wouldn't see it. The wood just didn't feel magical enough that day.

After tea came the very best thing of all. Decorating the Christmas tree.

Carl opened the shoe boxes where the decorations were kept. Inside all was gleaming and glittery — frosted baubles, heaps of tinsel, brightly painted wooden toys on golden loops of string. Carl took one silver star and fastened it on top of the little fir tree that Mr Berry had planted in the pot at the front door. It would be the first thing he saw when he came home.

Once the tree was finished, they stood on chairs to fasten up the paper chains and

put sprigs of holly behind the picture frames.

Now, at last, Christmas was really here!

Carl's mother fetched a bottle of ginger wine and the Christmas cake. She had put the same dear old figures on top of the crisp white icing – a Father Christmas and his sleigh, and the little snow-covered cottage

that Carl had always imagined must be
Father Christmas's house.

Very carefully Carl's mother cut the first
slice. It was full of raisins and cherries, and
smelt heavenly. Carl put it on a plate by his
father's favourite chair, along with a glass of
ginger wine.

Then he and his mother tried a piece. It
was even more delicious than the mince pies.
Carl sipped excitedly at his ginger wine. He

didn't really like ginger wine, it was just a special Christmas thing to do, but he liked the glass, with its delicate stem that was nice to hold between his fingers.

'Bedtime!' smiled his mother, after a while.

'Not yet!' cried Carl. And he ran upstairs to fetch his mother's present and Mr Berry's present. He'd been hiding them in his hiking boots, one in each foot. He laid them carefully under the Christmas tree.

There were no surprises there for him, yet – but by tomorrow there would be, he was sure of that!

That night Carl had a dream. He dreamed he was on a great silver sledge racing faster than the speed of light down a sparkling snow slope. The sledge was drawn by a mighty reindeer. On and on they went until they left winter far behind. Then the reindeer disappeared, and the sledge became a huge blue and silver bird. With Carl clinging to its back it sped along through a woodland bursting with blossom. It was the most wonderful feeling in the world.

When Carl woke up the first light of Christmas Day was peeping in over the tops of the curtains.

He jumped out of bed, and started to put on his slippers and dressing-gown. If he didn't, his mother would only send him all the way back upstairs to fetch them. Even if it was Christmas.

Outside it was snowing again.

Suddenly Carl found himself staring out at one of the rooftops. It had marks on it. Almost as if a great sledge had been standing there during the night. Carl stared harder, his heart thumping. There were lots of little marks there, too. Surely, *surely*, they couldn't be hoof marks! But even as he stared they disappeared like magic under the softly falling snow.

Then he saw something else, something beyond the tall dark houses. For a moment he thought it was the little Father Christmas cottage on top of the Christmas cake.

But it wasn't. It was Mr Berry's ice-cream parlour, covered with snow.

He remembered Mr Berry sitting on the roof, mending the hole: 'I've been on rooftops before, my lad ...'

Down the steps shot Carl. He hung on to the banister at every turn, his dressing-gown whizzing out like wings.

Mr Berry was fast asleep in his favourite armchair, his feet in a bowl of steaming-hot water.

'Thanks for the red mittens, Carl!' he beamed sleepily. 'They're just the right colour!'

'I always thought Father Christmas had a beard!' Carl blurted out.

'Well!' exclaimed his father, struggling to sit up. 'I expect he does wear a beard, on Christmas Eve. As a disguise! After all, if he didn't, somebody might wake up and

recognize him. Imagine what it would be like for him if that happened!'

'People would pester him all year round,' said Carl slowly.

'Exactly!' declared his father. 'And then he wouldn't have any time at all to spend with his family. Happy Christmas, son!' And he flung his arms open wide to give Carl a great bear hug.

'Happy Christmas, you two!' smiled Carl's mother, coming in with a mug of tea for everyone.

Carl ran to give her a hug, too – and then he saw it. Standing beside the Christmas tree. A beautiful blue and silver racing cycle.

'Ten-speed?' Carl whispered.

'Ten-speed!' replied his father, smiling.

'You guessed right, then,' said Carl.

'Let's open the other presents, too!' cried Carl's mother, kneeling down in front of the Christmas tree in her pretty pink dressing-gown. 'This present must be the smallest of all, and it's for me! I wonder what it is?'

It was the china thimble that Carl had bought her, and she thought it was beautiful. Especially the tiny pink rose.

Chapter Nine

Soon after Christmas the snow began to melt
and Andrew Brimblecombe came round to
admire Carl's new bike. They pleaded with
their mothers to let them ride to school
every day, once all the snow had gone. After
a long talk and a cup of tea the two mothers
said that they could, as there were no main
roads between where they lived and the
school.

In the garden all Mr Berry's bulbs began
to come up, daffodils, dainty snowdrops,
and crowds of crocuses. In the pot where the
little fir tree stood, clusters of yellow
primroses appeared. They made the pot look
like a crock of gold. As for the little pear tree,

it had become a cloud of snow-white
blossom.

Then one day, at the end of May, Mr
Berry stood up after breakfast, cleared his
throat, and said, 'Well, today's the day!'

'What for?' asked Carl, his heart pounding.

'Getting the ice-cream parlour ready for

summer!' replied Mr Berry, diving into the broom cupboard for all the cleaning equipment.

Then off they drove to the park, with the mop and broom sticking out of the back window of the little red car. Carl's mother decided to stay behind and put her feet up for a while. She had a lot of knitting to do.

Soon came the lovely moment when Mr Berry took the first board off the first window, and the sunshine flooded back into the little hut. They carried all the dear old tables and chairs outside to wash, and shook the dust off the parasols. Then they cleaned and polished until the little ice-cream parlour sparkled from top to toe.

'Next Saturday!' said Mr Berry afterwards, mopping his brow.

'Next Saturday!' said Carl.

That evening they spread newspaper all over the kitchen table and painted a big poster to hang on the park gates. It said:

MR BERRY'S ICE-CREAM PARLOUR
OPENING NEXT SATURDAY
COME AND TRY THE MYSTERIOUS NEW
FLAVOUR!

'What mysterious new flavour?' asked
Carl.

'Never you mind!' laughed his father.

Something else special happened that week. Something long-awaited and very special indeed. It meant that on opening day Carl's mother was sitting under one of the parasols pushing a shiny new pram backwards and forwards. Inside it, sound asleep with her thumb in her mouth, was Carl's chubby baby sister, her cheeks as soft and pink as rosebuds.

'What shall we call her?' smiled Carl's mother.

'Fatso!' said Mr Berry.

'Nicola!' said Carl.

'Rose!' said his mother.

So they called her Nicola Rose. Or Fatso, for short.

As for Mr Berry's mysterious new flavour, he called it 'Carl's Christmas Surprise', and everyone who tasted it thought it was Mr Berry's best ice-cream ever. But they couldn't decide what it actually tasted of. Some people thought it tasted of pear drops, others of cinnamon, while others thought they could taste a faint flavour of blackberries. But they all agreed on one thing. It melted on their tongue like snowflakes.

Andrew Brimblecombe thought the 'surprise' bit meant Carl's ten-speed racer.

Carl knew better.